HISTORIC TEXAS

Book of Days

Yvonne Bruce *and* Ann Bruce Hénaff

BRIGHT SKY PRESS

DEDICATION

*To LNB, whose idea it was to come to Texas, and EMO,
who followed some years thereafter.*

YB, ABH

BRIGHT SKY PRESS
Box 416
Albany, Texas 76430

10   9   8   7   6   5   4   3   2   1

Library of Congress Cataloging-in-Publication Data

Bruce, Yvonne, 1920–
     Historic Texas book of days / Yvonne Bruce and Ann Bruce Hénaff.
          p. cm.
     Includes bibliographical references.
     ISBN-13: 978-1-931721-96-7 (alk. paper)
     ISBN-10: 1-931721-96-3 (alk. paper)
Texas—History—Miscellanea. 2. Texas—Social life and customs—Miscellanea.
          3. Seasons—Texas—Miscellanea. 4. Cookery—Texas—Miscellanea. 5. Popular
          culture—Texas—Miscellanea. I. Hénaff, Ann Bruce, 1952– II. Title.

     F386.6.B78 2008
     976.4'06—dc22
                                                                            2007036349

Book and cover design by Isabel Lasater Hernandez
Edited by Dixie Nixon
Printed in China through Asia Pacific Offset

This book belongs to

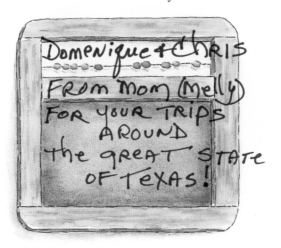

Domenique & Chris
From Mom (Melly)
FoR YouR TRIPS
AROUND
THE GREAT STATE
OF TEXAS!

PREFACE

*I*t is the desire of the Authors, while not discouraging the progressive spirit of the age, to temper it with affectionate feelings towards what was poetical and elevated, honest and of good report, in our State during the 19th and early 20th centuries.

The Book of Days is designed to consist of:
1. Phaenomena connected with the Seasonal Changes;
2. Articles of Popular Art and Architecture, of an entertaining character;
3. Notions and Observances connected with Culinary Matters; and
4. Curious, Fugitive, and Inedited Pieces.

We have done our best, with the means and opportunities at our disposal, to produce a work answering this plan, calculated to improve while it entertains, and mingling the agreeable with the instructive. In this they meanwhile rest, the Gentle Reader's Humble Servants,

Yvonne Bruce and Ann Bruce Hénaff

GARDEN CALENDAR*

Pecan orchard near the Colorado River

From December 25th to February 15th is our coldest weather. See that plants have sufficient protection and that they are not too dry, or too damp, or too close. Give as much air and sunshine as possible—do not be afraid of a little frost on the plants.

Now is the time, if not done before, to break up the ground. Loose soil is like a sponge, capable of absorbing and retaining the winter's rain until the summer's drouth. After freezing, turn it over again. Frost and ice will disintegrate it better than all the implements ever invented, and help to destroy insects.

In the orchard and flower garden, continue to plant and prune. Onions, salsify, spinach, parsnips, leeks or hardy flowery seeds can yet be planted.

onion

salsify

spinach

parsnips

1

2

3

4

5

6

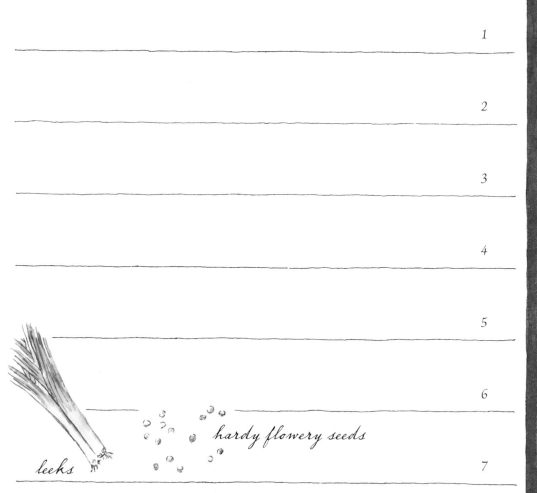

hardy flowery seeds

leeks

7

*The Garden Calendar first appeared in *Burke's Texas Almanac and Immigrant's Handbook for 1879.* Advice is given for the Dallas area each month, to be modified for other regions.

Four Patch

Nine Patch

Mama would card cotton and stack it on one of our chairs. When the chair was full, there was enough batting for a quilt.
—Annie Keeler

In early Texas, an entire quilting culture grew up around cotton. Homespun cloth, batting, and thread all came from cotton that was grown on or near the family farm.

Simple patterns such as the four patch, nine patch, Irish chain, and basket were favored for everyday quilts and for use by beginners. They were easily stitched together whenever a few moments could be spared from other chores.

A girl traditionally made a dozen quilt tops before her wedding. The bride's quilt, often all white, was usually stitched with hearts or roses, using her best skills, nicest materials, and most carefully planned design. When she was ready to marry, she held a quilting bee to quilt the tops in her hope chest.

Quilting bees were one of the main social events in those days. The women spent the day sewing, and in the evening, the men were invited for supper and dancing.

Spool

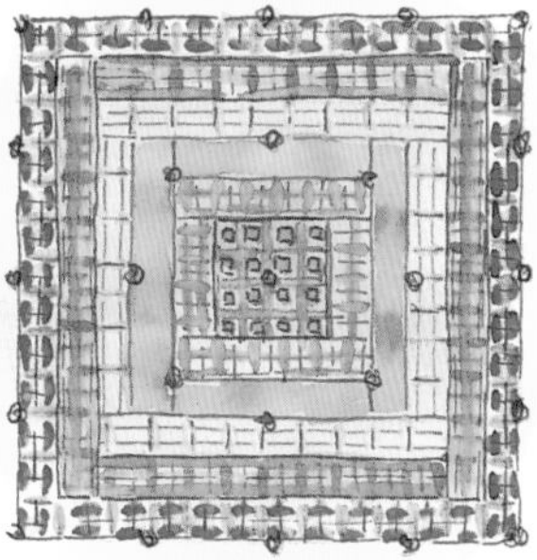

Log Cabin, one of the most abstract designs in quiltmaking

Courthouse Steps

8

9

10

11

12

13

14

Double Irish Chain

This presentation quilt was begun by Harriet Spicer before the birth of her first child, and completed two years after his arrival. Cross-stitched into one corner of the quilt is this inscription: *Presented to William Porter Spicer by his mother, Harriet S F Spicer April 1st 1854*. Another corner has a bit of motherly advice: *Patience Industry Economy Prudence Ingenuity, Encouraged*. William Porter Spicer and his quilt homesteaded in South Dakota during the 1880s, and later came to Texas in 1910 with a land party to develop the Rio Grande Valley.

Patience   Industry   Economy
Prudence   Ingenuity, Encouraged.

15

16

17

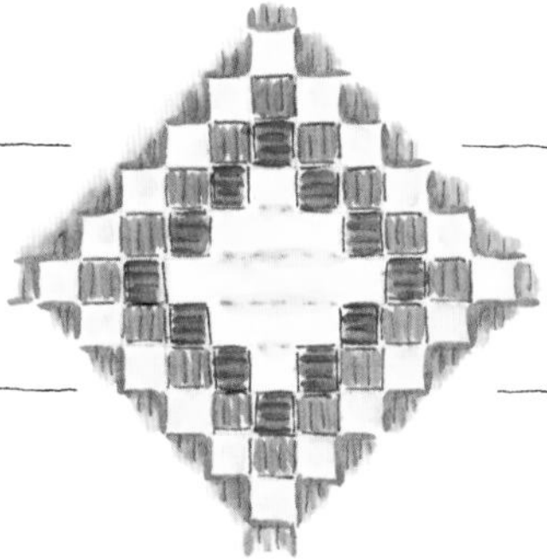

18

Triple Irish Chain

19

20

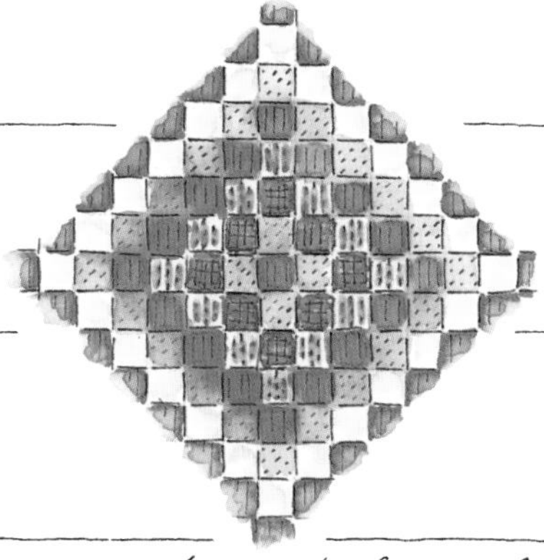

21

Trip Around the World

22

Flower Basket

23

24

25

Rosebud

26

27

28

North Carolina Lily

29

Rose Wreath 30

31

Love Apple,
or tomato, was
thought to be inedible
prior to 1850.

GARDEN CALENDAR

    Plant seeds of peas, turnips, carrots, beets, lettuce, radishes, cress or pepper grass, early corn, and Irish potatoes, and protect if necessary. Set out the main crop of cauliflower, lettuce, beets, celery, onions, endive, if the weather is favorable, from plants in cold frames. Reserve a few plants for fear of loss. Make horseradish and asparagus beds. Plant tomato seeds in cold frames, and protect with glass; or sow in a box in a south window.

    Continue work in orchard and flower garden, as long as sap is not flowing. Divide and set out chrysanthemums, verbenas, carnations, tritomas, iris, lychnis, hemerocalis, rosemary, sage, thyme, &c. Set phlox and other hardy annuals; lillies and Dutch bulbs should now be well established.

A well-maintained asparagus bed can produce for 10—15 years.

1

2

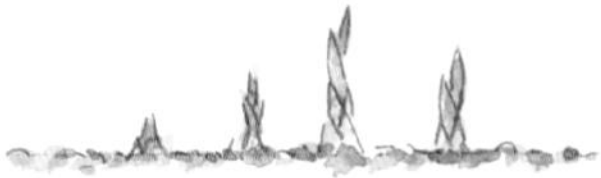

Lillies and Dutch bulbs

3

4

5

6

7

The Keidel House, built of cut limestone from local quarries,
stands on one of the original town lots.

Fredericksburg, named in honor of Prince Frederick of Prussia, was established in 1846. It was the second settlement after New Braunfels to be organized by the Adelsverein, also known as the German Emigration Company. Under their terms, each settler received one town lot and ten acres of farmland nearby. Snug houses, well-tended dairies, and tidy vegetable gardens were standard practice, and rumor has it that barbecue had its beginning in German smokehouses.

Ocular attic vent

Cornerstone, front façade

8

9

10

11

12

13

14

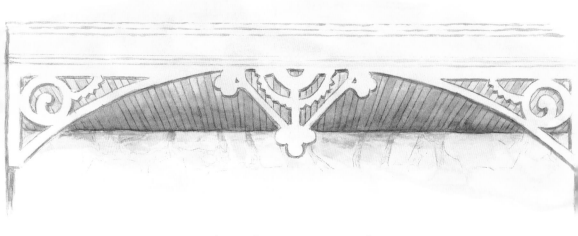

*The lacework look of the gingerbread trim sets
this porch apart from others found in Fredericksburg.*

Mr. and Mrs. George Wahrmund acquired this building in 1876, and Mrs. Wahrmund set up a millinery and dressmaking shop in part of the first floor. She and her husband, along with their three daughters, lived in the rest of the house. According to Elise Kowert, in *Old Homes and Buildings of Fredericksburg*, the George Wahrmund family was "socially and culturally inclined." One can just imagine the creations that sailed out of her shop during the latter part of the nineteenth century.

On the facing page is a replica of the Vereinskirche, or Community Church. Built by the first settlers in 1847, it served as a church, school, fortress, and meeting hall.

15

16

17

18

19

The Vereinskirche was nicknamed
the Coffee Mill Church, because
of its octagonal shape.

20

21

From February through October, East Texas woods and wetlands are abloom with a variety of unusual native plants. Here are just a few:

Scarlet Catchfly

(*Silene subciliata*)
Blooms July to October, woodlands and sandhills.

Bog Coneflower

(*Rudbeckia scabrifolia*)
Blooms June to September, bogs and forests.

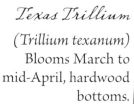

Texas Golden Glade Cress

(*Leavenworthia texana*)
Blooms March to May, wet glades.

White Fire-wheel

(*Gaillardia aestivalis var. winkleri*)
Blooms February to September, woodlands.

Texas Trillium

(*Trillium texanum*)
Blooms March to mid-April, hardwood bottoms.

Neches River Rose-mallow

(*Hibiscus dasycalyx*)
Blooms June to August, swamps and woodlands.

Bogs are frequent, and not a little dangerous, as there are scarcely any visible signs of them, and if you are unlucky enough to get well into one, the chances are rather against your soon getting out again.
—Matilda Charlotte Houstoun,
Texas and the Gulf of Mexico; or,
Yachting in the New World, 1845

22

23

24

25

26

27

28/29

Prairie Dawn (Hymenoxys texana)
Blooms March to April, coastal prairie grasslands.

Plant a row of beans every two weeks until early June. From May on, plant in half shade. Add stakes as soon as plants are a few inches high; small twigs at the base of the stakes will help them climb more easily.

This is a month of great anxiety. We must risk planting early, and yet the frosty winds linger after snow and ice are gone.

As the weather moderates, plant pole and dwarf snap beans, okra, squash, cucumbers and cantaloupes. Set out tomatoes, egg plants, peppers, watermelons, butter beans and southern peas a little later. Plant asparagus seeds—it does well on rich prairie soil. Keep the hoe and cultivator moving all the time.

Shrimp Gumbo

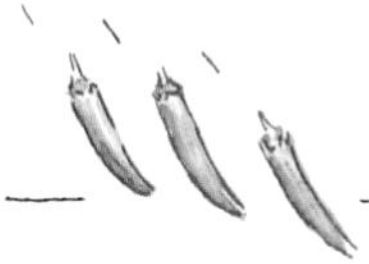

3 cups okra, chopped

2 onions, chopped

3 pods garlic, chopped

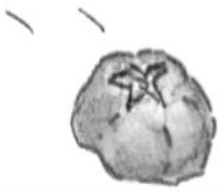

4 cups tomatoes, chopped

Red pepper

1 bay leaf

2 pounds shrimp, peeled and deveined

Sauté onions and okra in a small amount of oil. Add remaining ingredients (except for shrimp), and cook for 10 minutes, adding water as needed. Add shrimp, cook an additional 5 minutes. Serve with rice.

1

2

3

4

5

6

7

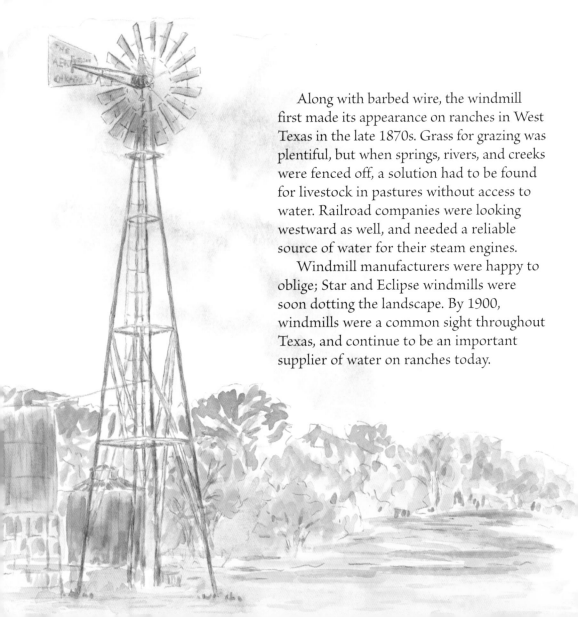

Along with barbed wire, the windmill first made its appearance on ranches in West Texas in the late 1870s. Grass for grazing was plentiful, but when springs, rivers, and creeks were fenced off, a solution had to be found for livestock in pastures without access to water. Railroad companies were looking westward as well, and needed a reliable source of water for their steam engines.

Windmill manufacturers were happy to oblige; Star and Eclipse windmills were soon dotting the landscape. By 1900, windmills were a common sight throughout Texas, and continue to be an important supplier of water on ranches today.

8

9

10

11

12

A vane directs the wheel into the wind.

13

14

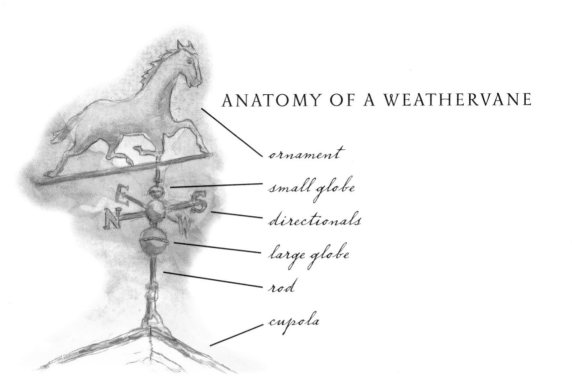

ANATOMY OF A WEATHERVANE

ornament

small globe

directionals

large globe

rod

cupola

Always pointing into the wind, the weather vane has been part of the landscape for centuries. Its heyday in America was in the 19th century, when three-dimensional designs such as the one above were inspired by Currier and Ives prints of famous race horses. Elaborate Victorian weather vanes followed in the last decades of the 19th century. After 1900, simpler styles of architecture were reflected in silhouette weather vanes such as the rooster on the facing page.

15

16

17

18

19

20

*Vernal, or spring equinox: March 20
or 21, according to the year.*
        —*The Old Farmer's 2007 Almanac*

21

22
_____

23
_____

24
_____

25
_____

26
_____

27
_____

28
_____

29

30

31

GARDEN CALENDAR

At this season the cold rain ceases, and we have some dry weather. But the diligent gardener has his ground in such fine condition that his plants do not feel it. Set out a liberal supply of tomatoes early in the month. It is our leading summer vegetable. Also, set out early sweet potatoes, egg plants and peppers. Set out lettuce and plant radishes in a rich, cool spot. Plant more cucumbers. Keep the cultivator and the hoe continually moving.

Sow seeds in bed for fall planting of cabbages, celery, asparagus, leeks and onions for sets, and collards to be set out in June. Also sow seeds, or divide old plants, of sage, thyme, rosemary, chrysanthemums, carnations, and pinks.

Now is a good time to set a lawn with Bermuda grass—a few roots, two or four feet apart, will soon make the most beautiful sod in the world.

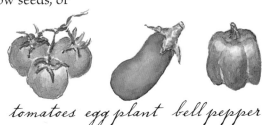

tomatoes egg plant bell pepper

carnations and pinks

1

2

Plant cotton during the first full moon following Easter, or around April 1st. Harvest will be in 90 days.

3

4

sage   rosemary   thyme

5

6

7

*Cotton plantation and original home (c. 1844) of Anson Jones,
last president of the Republic of Texas*

The dog-trot structure with a central breezeway provides shade and ventilation during the hot summer months. Buildings of this type often faced south, minimizing the effect of the summer sun high in the sky at midday, and allowing the afternoon sun of winter to warm the interior. This building is now part of the Barrington Living History Farm, located in Washington-on-the-Brazos.

We began to raise cotton in the year
1886 on the prairie. The people thought
at first that it would not grow on the
prairies, and so for years the section where
the cotton was raised in this country was
in the bottoms near the rivers. We first
tried the small patches and as they did
well, we then planted larger acreage.
—Amelia Steward Christoffer,
A Legacy of Words, Texas Women's
Stories 1850–1920

8

9

10

11

12

13

14

HILL COUNTRY WILDFLOWERS

Indian Blanket
(Gaillardia pulchella)
Blooms May
through July.

Bluebonnet
(Lupinus texensis)
Peak blooming period
is mid-April.

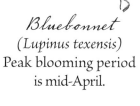

Basketflower
(Centaurea americana)
Blooms May–June.

Indian
Paintbrush
(Castilleja spp.)
Peak blooming
period is mid-April.

Blue-star
(Amsonia ciliata)
Blooms March–June.

Texas Thistle
(Cirsium texanum)
Blooms
April–August.

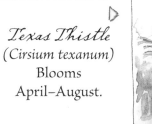

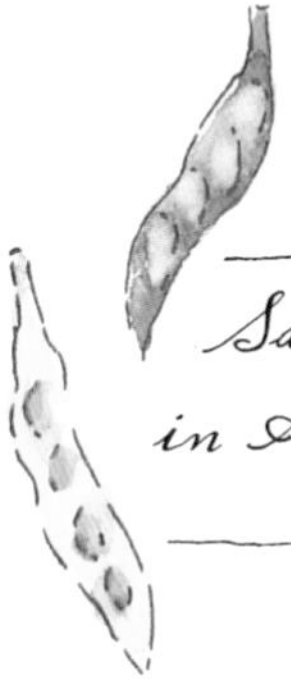

15

Save bluebonnet seeds, and sow in August or September.

16

17

18

19

20

Everyone knows that Texas is the wildflower garden of the world.
—Davy Crockett, in a letter written to his children from the Alamo, *Houston's Forgotten Heritage*

21

CATTLE DRIVES

Cattle drives in Texas began during the Reconstruction period following the Civil War, when low beef prices encouraged ranchers to look elsewhere for new markets. Trails such as the Chisholm and Goodnight-Loving were established, and over the next 25 years, roughly 10 million longhorns were driven to railheads in Kansas and Missouri for shipment back East, and to markets in New Mexico, Colorado, and Wyoming.

A traveling herd consisted of about 2,500 head of cattle, controlled by two point men in front, two press men on the sides, and several others to round up stragglers. Each cowboy had five or six horses; one was always saddled, in case of stampedes or Indian attacks. With herds traveling an average of twelve miles a day, cattle drives could last from six weeks to five months.

The chuck wagon was invented by Charles Goodnight, and it became an integral part of cattle drives. It was often made from an old army wagon, with a chuck box installed at the back. The chuck box had shelves and drawers for storing utensils and supplies. A hinged door on the back held everything in place while traveling, and upon arrival, let down to form a table for food preparation. Standard fare was beef or other available meat, pinto beans, and biscuits, with an occasional cobbler or pie as a special treat.

The cowboys would ride around the herd day and night, and to keep the herd quiet they would sing the cowboy songs. This had a soothing effect on the herds, and they seldom had a stampede.
—Amelia Steward Christoffer, *A Legacy of Words, Texas Women's Stories 1850–1920*

22

23

24

25

26

27

The longhorn's hardiness was well-suited for the semidesert 28
regions of West Texas and the South Texas brush country.

Pinto Beans

serves 6

6 slices bacon
1 onion
2 cloves garlic
1¹/₂ cups pinto beans
5 cups water
Chili powder to taste
1 tablespoon brown sugar
1 25 oz. jar tomato sauce (optional)
Salt to taste

Chop bacon, onion, and garlic, and brown in Dutch oven. Wash beans, add along with 3 cups water, chili powder, and brown sugar. Bring to a boil, then reduce heat and cover. Simmer for 3–4 hours, or until beans are soft. Check every so often, and add water as needed. Add tomato sauce if desired, and salt to taste.

Drop Biscuits

¼ c. oil   2 c. flour
1 c. milk   3 t. baking powder

Preheat oven to 350°. Coat an 8-inch cast iron skillet with oil, and set in oven to heat while mixing batter. Mix oil and milk, sift in dry ingredients. Stir with a fork just until moistened. Scoop a spoonful of batter and place it in the skillet. Continue, working from the outside edges into the middle. Cook until golden, about 15-20 minutes. Serve immediately.
Makes 8-10 medium biscuits.

A pot of strong coffee was always
ready to 'quicken the spirit and make
the heart lightsome.'
—*Eats, a Folk History of Texas Foods*

GARDEN CALENDAR

Lovely May is here, with its flowers, early fruits and vegetables. The gardener is delighted with his success, and the prospect ahead is cheering. But there is no time for rest. The soil must be continually stirred, not only to kill the weeds, but to keep it loose and sponge-like, ready to absorb and hold the dews and rain against the coming drouth.

For summer use, continue to plant Southern peas and beans of all kinds, beets, carrots, melons of all kinds, and okra; set out tomato plants and main crop of sweet potatoes.

For use this fall, plant in latter part of this month, or early in June, snap beans and Southern peas, cucumbers for pickles, parsnips, salsify, beets, rutabaga or Sweedish turnips, and set out cabbages; also collards for winter use.

The small tendril that attaches the watermelon to the vine dries up when it is ripe.
When thumped, a ripe watermelon produces a hollow, dull sound, as opposed to a ringing, sharp sound from one that is immature.

1

rutabaga   Sweedish turnip

2

3

4

5

6

7

SOUTHERN MAGNOLIA
(Magnolia grandiflora)

The cup-shaped flowers have a citrusy fragrance.

    This native evergreen tree is found along streams and rivers in East Texas. It gives its name to the family Magnoliaceae.

    Basic needs: full sun to partial shade, adequate water. It does best in rich, well-drained, acidic soils.

8

9

Stamens

10

Buds appear at the tip of a branch,
wrapped in a bud scale.

11

12

13

14

Seed pod

GULF COAST WATERBIRDS

Brown Pelican
(*Pelecanus occidentalis*)

American
Oystercatcher
(*Haematopus*
palliatus)

Long-billed Curlew
(*Numenius americanus*)

Black Skimmer
(*Rynchops niger*)

Black-necked Stilt
(*Himantopus mexicanus*)

Great Egret
(*Ardea alba*)

15

16

17

Roseate Spoonbills
(Platalea ajaja)

18

19

20

Whooping Crane
(Grus americana)

21

EARLY KITCHEN GARDENS

Settlers from the Austin colony who arrived in 1832 started their vegetable and herb gardens soon after arrival. Beets, onions, "raddishes," okra, white mustard, parsnips, peas, and beans were mentioned in early accounts, as were parsley, sage, and "thime."

The checkerboard layout, alternating squares of herbs with paving stones or bricks, is interesting and practical, especially when located near the kitchen door.

Parsley
(Petroselium crispum) prefers a sunny location and rich, moist soil.

Garden sage
(Salvia officinalis) will grow in any well-drained soil in a sunny location.

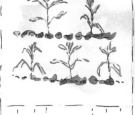

Garlic
(Allium sativum) prefers a sunny location and well-drained soil.

Rosemary
(Rosemarinus officinalis) prefers light, dry soil in full sun.

Pepper family
(Capsicum annuum) includes pimiento, jalapeño, and bell peppers.

Common thyme
(Thymus vulgaris) is an evergreen perennial that prefers sun.

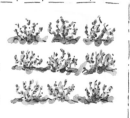

Sow seed and transplant with a waxing, never waning, moon.

22

Garlic clears a muddled brain.
—Eats, a Folk History of Texas Foods

23

24

25

26

Save dried stems of herbs such as
rosemary, lavender, lemon verbena,   27
and thyme. Bundle together, and
when winter comes, add
to a fire in the fireplace   28
to scent the room.

The mint family includes wild mint (Mentha Canadénsis), *peppermint* (M. pipérita), *and spearmint* (M. viridis).

Mint grows best in fertile, well-draining soil, with consistent moisture and partial shade. It is well-suited to a wall facing north. It can be grown from seed, from plant cuttings rooted in water, or from root division. It can also be started indoors in a pot placed near a sunny window.

lemon   *mint*   *iced tea with*   *sugar*
quarters   *sprigs*   *iced tea spoon*

Mint develops more flavor when grown beside camomile.

East Texas Mint Julep

serves 4

1 cup sugar
1 cup water
8–10 sprigs of fresh mint
Cracked ice
Bourbon

Make a simple syrup of sugar and water.
Stir well, and bring to a boil. Let cool.

Crush a few sprigs of mint all around the inside of four
cups. Discard sprigs. Fill with cracked ice, and pour in the
desired amount of bourbon. Allow the bourbon to become
thoroughly chilled, then add 2–4 tablespoons of the sugar
syrup. Let stand for a few minutes without stirring.
Garnish with a sprig of mint, and serve immediately.

GARDEN CALENDAR

Summer is coming upon us fast, and any work neglected last month must be attended to at once. Take advantage of cloudy or rainy days for sowing and planting, for July and August will be too dry and hot for such work.

Be sure and get a full crop of sweet potatoes. Cure onions in the sun—Irish potatoes in the shade. Store the latter in a cool, airy place, or in boxes of dry earth.

The "budding" of roses and fruit trees should now be attended to. Grape vines laid down in the soil now will be rooted by frost. Roses can also be propagated in this manner, first tonguing the layered limb.

It will be necessary to employ shade and more water, especially for celery.

Layerage works well for jasmine, clematis, wisteria, and azaleas.

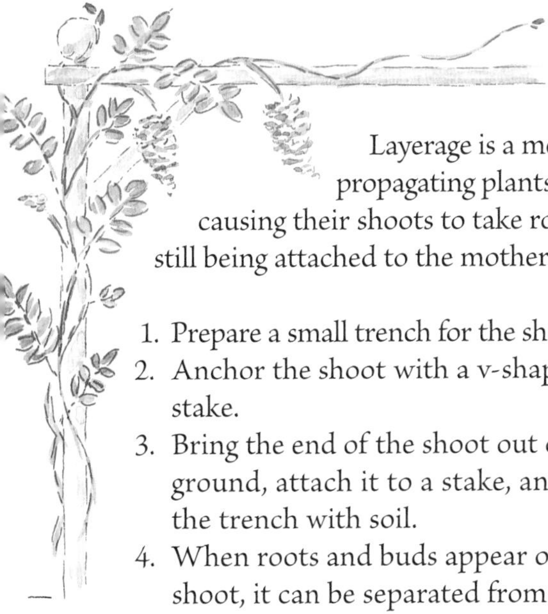

Layerage is a method of propagating plants by causing their shoots to take root while still being attached to the mother plant.

1. Prepare a small trench for the shoot.
2. Anchor the shoot with a v-shaped stake.
3. Bring the end of the shoot out of the ground, attach it to a stake, and fill the trench with soil.
4. When roots and buds appear on the shoot, it can be separated from the mother plant.

1

2

3

4

5

6

7

Cure onions in the sun,
Irish potatoes in the shade.

The milk was put in the crockery churn and after some time spent in churning the dasher up and down, the cream became butter and could be scooped into molds for eating and cooking. Grandpa Clark was good to come and help with the churning, but we kids sometimes took turns at this job.

—Kathryn Cavitt's journal

During the nineteenth century, dairy cattle in Texas were owned primarily by small farmers and individuals. The latter were families living both in town and out in the country, who kept milk cows for their personal use.

By 1900, a small number of creameries were in operation, and in 1928 the first cheese plant was established. Over time, butter and cheese production declined and were replaced by ice cream. Blue Bell Creameries, located in Brenham, is a prime example. It began making butter in 1907, then added ice cream production in 1911. Flavors included vanilla, chocolate, strawberry, and buttered pecan. The most popular flavor was vanilla, which still holds true today.

Guernsey

Dairy farms have always been located in the eastern third of the state, because of rich pasture land and more abundant water. Beginning in the 1880s, Jerseys and Holsteins were the two main breeds: Jerseys, which produce a richer milk that is used for cream, butter, or cheese; and Holsteins, because of their large capacity for milk production. Guernseys were introduced in the early 20th century; they produce milk similar to that of the Jersey.

Jersey

Holstein

We usually had at least one milk cow which provided milk for our family. My brother Clark learned to milk the cows early in his life, and he could squirt a stream of milk directly from the cow's udder to the open mouth of a cat awaiting nearby.

—Kathryn Cavitt's journal

8

9

10

11

12

13

14

Milk was also delivered early in the morning, and left on the porch.

FOR YOUR PROTECTION
Raw Milk
E. W. MC PHETERS
JERSEY
MILK
PULL HERE
PHONE 74-2
DAIRY SERVICE

VISITING

White wicker chairs invite visitors to come and sit a spell.

In the summer months, the front porch, often extending across the length of the house, was used as an outdoor living room. In southeast Texas, porches were opened to the south and east, to take advantage of prevailing Gulf breezes. A back porch, usually near the kitchen, was used for more practical matters such as churning butter or preparing vegetables.

What to serve? Here is a recipe from Aunt/Great-Aunt Florence:

Plain Cake
1 cup sugar, 2 eggs, 1 teaspoon butter, 1½ cup flour, ½ cup milk, 1 heaping teaspoon baking powder. Bake in 2 layers filled between and frosted with filling made thus: 1 cup sugar, ½ cup milk, a piece of butter the size of an egg. Boil this 10 minutes, flavor to taste. Makes a nice cake for tea.

Miss Florence Clark, *A Book of Tested Recipes Arranged by the Woman's Missionary Society of the Methodist Church, McGregor, Texas, 1920*

There is little if anything more to be said of these unceremonious but exceedingly pleasant affairs. A greeting, a cup of tea, a little harmless gossip, a farewell, and that is all.
—Frances Stevens, *The Usages of the Best Society*, 1884

1 5

1 6

1 7

1 8

1 9

Summer solstice: June 20 or 21, depending on the year.
—The Old Farmer's 2007 Almanac

2 0

2 1

Gazebo, Magnolia

During the Victorian period, the garden became an outdoor gathering place for family and friends. Garden structures such as gazebos and arbors provided places to sit in the shade and visit. Because of their open sides, placement was important, in order to take advantage of the view.

Nosegay

Fan

22

23

24

25

26

27

28

SUMMERTIME

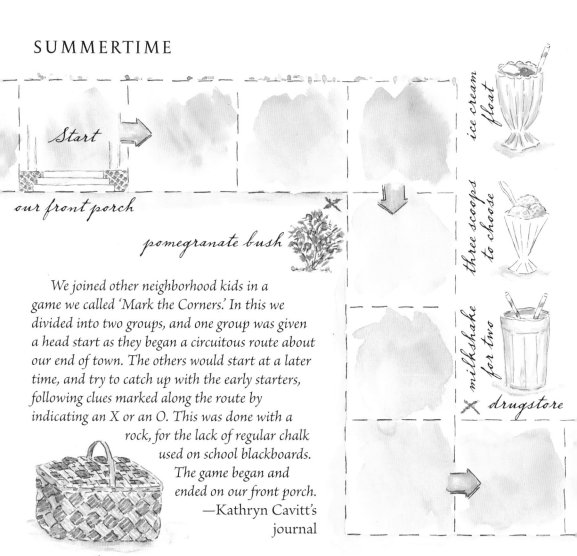

Start

our front porch

pomegranate bush

ice cream float

three scoops to choose

milkshake for two

drugstore

We joined other neighborhood kids in a game we called 'Mark the Corners.' In this we divided into two groups, and one group was given a head start as they began a circuitous route about our end of town. The others would start at a later time, and try to catch up with the early starters, following clues marked along the route by indicating an X or an O. This was done with a rock, for the lack of regular chalk used on school blackboards. The game began and ended on our front porch.
—Kathryn Cavitt's journal

picnic basket (we wonder what's inside)

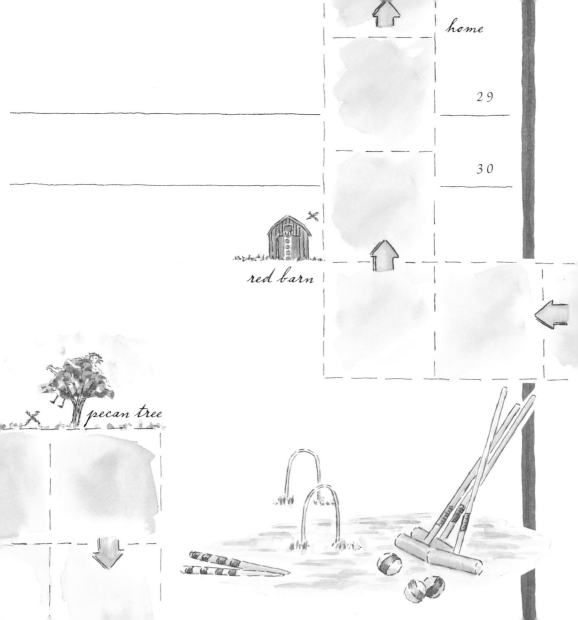

home

29

30

red barn

pecan tree

GARDEN CALENDAR

Our tables are loaded with every kind of fruit and vegetables. Planting for fall may continue, if the season is favorable. Southern peas, snap beans, watermelons, rutabagas, are the most reliable.

The weather will be hot the last of July, but we must not cease cultivation. Loose soil is the best mulch, and better than watering.

For seeds, always save the finest and earliest specimens. Tomato, lettuce, squash, spinach, cucumber, cantaloupe, parsley, endive, and bean seeds can be saved with proper care without degeneration; while watermelons, onions, leeks, collards, okra, corn, pepper, mustard, &c., are really improved. Also, save flower seeds.

Beans and peas should be gathered in bunches and stored in the attic or any well-ventilated place. Leave peas, etc., in their pods.

Keep a sunny part of the garden with good soil for plants grown for seed. Reserve a row or two for each variety.

Once the seeds are dry, collect in an envelope or cloth bag. Label with the name of the plant and date of harvest.

Summer Ragoût   1

freshly picked peas   2

potatoes   3

small
carrots 
4

and onions   5

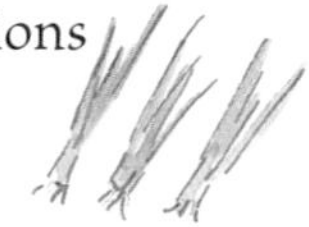

with a bit of meat (pork,
veal, or mutton) if desired

6

Sauté meat in a small
amount of oil, add other
ingredients one by one.   7
Add water as needed,
and cook until tender.

BY THE SEA

The Texas coastline stretches over 624 miles.

European discovery of the Gulf of Mexico is credited to Sebastián de Ocampo, a Spanish navigator who sailed around Cuba in 1508–09, and reported the presence of a body of water that lay beyond the island. The first map to represent this "hidden sea" and its littoral was completed by Don Alonzo Alvarez de Piñeda following his voyage there in 1519. Subsequent Spanish and French expeditions in the 16th and 17th centuries contributed additional information on coastal features, water depth, and bottom composition, the latter important in determining suitability of anchorage.

In 1719, Texas is mentioned in writing for the first time as "Los Teijas" on a map produced by French cartographer Guillaume Delisle. In the 19th and early 20th centuries, additional information on prevailing currents and fishery resources became available as well.

When keeping a log, the state of the sea is expressed by the following system of symbols:

B Broken or irregular sea
C Chopping, short, or cross sea
G Ground swell
H Heavy sea

L Long rolling sea
M Moderate sea or swell
R Rough sea
S Smooth sea
T Tide rips

—Nathaniel Bowditch,
American Practical Navigator, 1926

Map courtesy Texas General Land Office

Signal Flag Basics

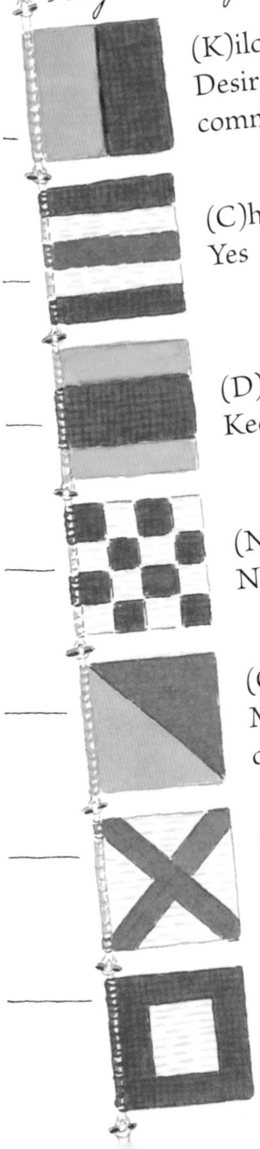

(K)ilo
Desire to
communicate

8

(C)harlie
Yes

In fair weather,
prepare for foul.
—The Old Farmer's
2007 Almanac

9

(D)elta
Keep clear

10

(N)ovember
No

11

(O)scar
Man
overboard

12

(V)ictor
Require
assistance

13

(P)apa
About
to sail

14

Port Isabel Light

Located in Texas' southernmost port, the Port Isabel Light began operation in 1853. Open to the public, the panoramic views are worth the climb.

Lydia Ann Light

Lydia Ann Light, named for the daughter of its first keeper, is located on Harbor Island, northwest of Aransas Pass. Not open to the public.

Matagorda Island Light

The first lighthouse built in Texas, its lamps were lit initially on December 21, 1852. It was constructed of iron plates that could be disassembled and moved. Open to the public.

Point Bolivar Light

Point Bolivar Light is located on the Bolivar Peninsula, at the eastern edge of Galveston Bay. The lighthouse was completed in the last days of 1852. Not open to the public.

TIME OF WATCH.		CONDITION OF LIGHT.	CONDITION OF FOG SIGNAL.
GOING ON.	LEAVING.		
12m	SR	No Light - due to heavy. vibration" Caused by Wind -	
SS	12m		
12m	SR	No Light due to plate glass blown out, Everything Wet & Covered With Water	
SS	12m		
12m	SR	"	

From the collection of the Calhoun County Museum

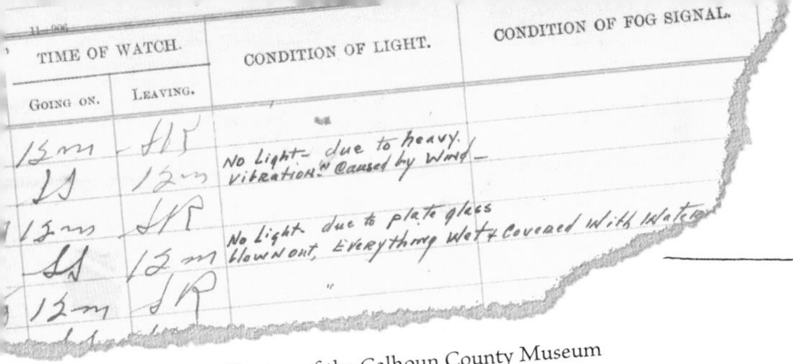

Logbook entries by keepers of the Matagorda Island lighthouse

15

16

17

18

19

20

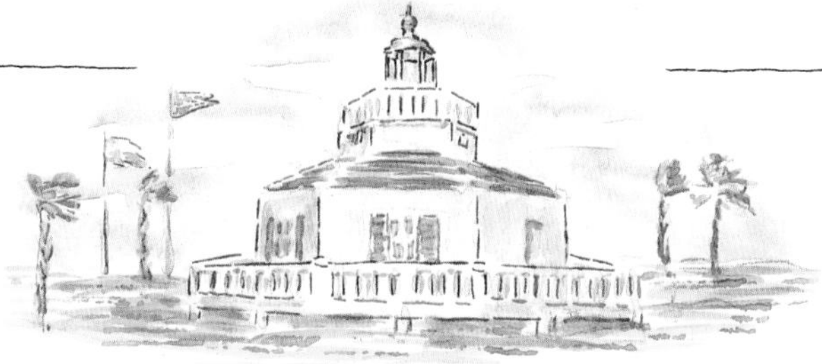

Halfmoon Reef Light

Halfmoon Reef is an oystershell shoal on the eastern side of Matagorda Bay. In 1858, the lighthouse's hexagonal structure was built on an iron screwpile foundation secured to the shoal. Now located in Port Lavaca. Open to the public.

21

SALTWATER FISH

More than 300 fish species have been identified off the Texas coast. Here is a sampling:

Tarpon
(Megalops atlanticus)

Red Snapper
(Lutjanus campechanus)

Atlantic Croaker
(Micropogon undulatus)

Greater Amberjack
(Seriola dumerili)

Spotted Seatrout
(Cynoscion nebulosus)

Red Drum
(Sciaenops ocellatus)

King Mackerel
(Scomberomorus cavalla)

22

23

24

25

26

27

28

Southern Flounder
(Paralichthys lethostigma)

A SEASHELL SAMPLER

Shark Eye
(Neverita duplata)
It inhabits sandy beaches, gliding along just below the surface.

Lightning Whelk
(Busycon sinistrum)
The name comes from the lines on its shell that resemble lightning bolts. It is found only along the west coast of the Gulf of Mexico, and is the state shell of Texas.

Angel Wing
(Cyrtopleura costata)
A filter feeder, this burrowing clam adores mud flats.

Sundial
(Architectonica nobilis)
With spirals inside and out, this shell's design is one of the most intricate of all mollusks.

Sea Urchin
(Arbacia punctulata)
It lives among the rocks of jetties, and feeds mainly on algae. Adhesive tube feet help it to move around, and spines give protection from predators.

Turkey Wing
(Arca zebra)
Common to shallow rock reefs, this wing-shaped seashell has brown and white zebra stripes.

29

30

31

Sand Dollars

Among this collection of sand dollars, the Keyhole Sand Dollar (*Mellita quinquiesperforata*) with its five oblong slots is the only native Texan. All are found in sandy sediments just beyond the surf zone.

Atlantic Thorny Oyster

(*Spondylus americanus*) This ferocious-looking bivalve attaches itself to offshore reefs, living at depths ranging from intertidal down to 50 feet.

GARDEN CALENDAR

Our main crop of vegetables is partially exhausted, but the deficiency is compensated for by a liberal supply of fruits. If preparations for a fall garden have been neglected, delay no longer. A second spring can be added to our seasons by proper management.

kale   kohl rabi

If the weather continues hot and dry until the last of the month, sow a half crop of the following on top of the ground, viz: early and late rutabagas, turnips, kohl rabi, kale, borecole, lettuce, endive, mustard, radishes, carrots, &c.; and the following a little deeper: beans, parsnips, beets, onion seeds or sets, English peas and salsify.

Look after the seed-bed in dry weather, and see that it does not suffer from insects, or for want of water.

Store fruit in a cellar or other room where there is little variation in temperature.

When watering ...

The water should be at the same temperature as the air; leave it in the open air for several hours in a watering-can or barrel. In summer, water in the evening after sunset; in the spring and fall, water in the morning. Large vegetables should be watered at the base, smaller ones sprinkled with the rose attachment.

1

Bunches of grapes can be hung from the rafters.

2

3

4

5

Dry plums first in the sun,
and then in the oven when it 6
is still warm from baking.

7

A ROOF OVER MAMA'S HEAD

Log cabin, Wheelock, c. 1836

Ann and Andrew Cavitt and their seven sons came to Texas from Tennessee in 1835. Andrew died of yellow fever soon after arriving; Ann went ahead with their plans, and purchased land in Wheelock. In 1836, she and her sons moved into their first log cabin home.

*I have no widow's weeds to mourn him
in, and no time to dwell upon my grief.
Despite the tugging at my heart to be with
my people, I would not retrace our steps for
all the corn, cotton, and cattle in the state
of Coahuila and Texas. Andrew wished
earnestly to see his sons established in this
land, and it shall be so, by God's help.*
—Ann Cavitt's journal,
Stagecoach Inns of Texas

8

9

1 0

1 1

1 2

1 3

1 4

*A farm bell was used for calling
people to a meal, or for emergencies.*

Log cabin, Wheelock, seen from the side

The downstairs was used as a kitchen and dining area, and the loft above for sleeping quarters. Fire holes were cut between the logs for muskets and long rifles.

The cabin later served as a stagecoach stop on the Camino Real route between Nacogdoches and San Antonio.

The stage station was one big room made from cedar logs and would hold as many as six horses. They were kept there to change for fresh horses. The fresh horses were brought, and by the time they were changed the driver would call, 'All ready' and away they went.

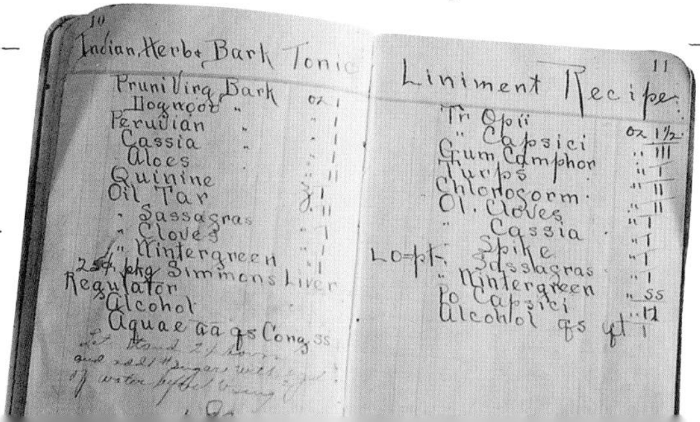

—Amelia Steward Christoffer,
A Legacy of Words, Texas Women's Stories 1850–1920

15

16

17

18

19

For horses that had just arrived, a rubdown was always welcome.

20

21

10
Indian Herb & Bark Tonic
Pruni Virg Bark oz 1
Dogwood " 1
Peruvian " 1
Cassia " 1
Aloes " 11
Quinine 3 1
Oil Tar 3 11
" Sassagras " 1
" Cloves " 1
" Wintergreen " 1
25¢ pkg Simmons Liver Regulator
Alcohol
Aquae aa qs Cong ss

11
Liniment Recipe
Tr Opii oz 1½
" Capsici " 111
Gum Camphor " 1
Turps " 11
Chloroform " 11
Ol. Cloves " 1
" Cassia " 1
Spike " 1
Sassagras " 1
" Wintergreen " 1
Po Capsici " ss
Alcohol qs qt 1

—*Recipe Book for Veterinary Medicines,*
Mills County Historical Museum

Stage Coach Inn, Chappell Hill, c. 1851

After Austin became the capital of Texas in 1846, travel by stagecoach between Austin, Houston, and Waco increased as the state developed. The Stage Coach Inn at Chappell Hill, built in Greek Revival style, became known for its comfortable accommodations and good food. An interesting architectural feature is the ornamental Greek-key frieze worked into the cornice.

22

23

24

25

26

27

28

For equine guests

Master builder Abner Cook used native limestone and Bastrop pine in the construction of this elegant country house.

Another Greek Revival structure is the Neill-Cochran House in Austin, built in 1855–56. Front and back parlors, dining room, and study open off either side of the central hall. High ceilings, as well as tall windows and a shady veranda on the east side, kept the house cool in the summer.

29

30

31

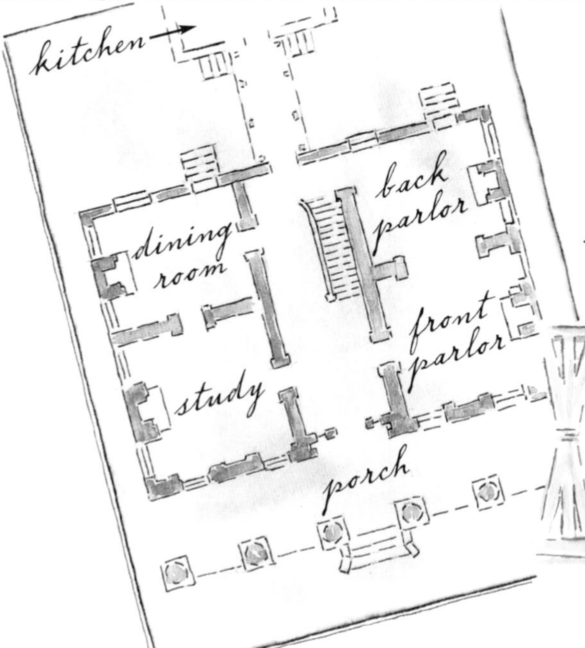

kitchen →

dining room

back parlor

study

front parlor

porch

Abner Cook's signature sheaves of wheat motif.

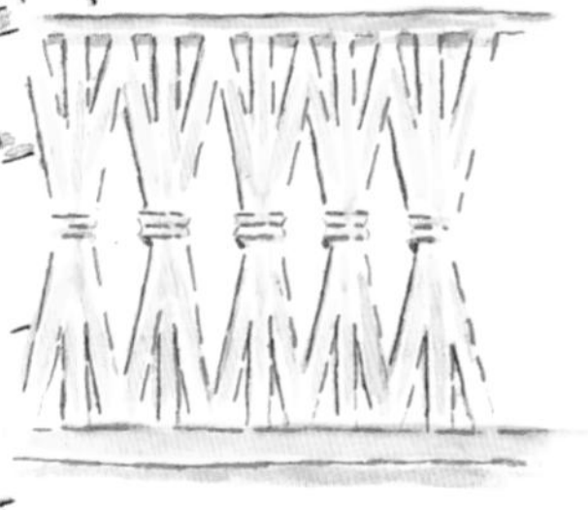

GARDEN CALENDAR

Rocky Mountain Douglas fir (Pseudotsuga menziesii var. glauca)

Eastern red-cedar (Juniperus virginiana)

Bald cypress (Taxodium distichum)

For the coming winter and spring, we must plant the following, about the middle of September, or first of October, viz: onions, leeks, parsnips, kale, borecole, rutabagas, salsify and spinach. Set out celery, and water and shade until established.

Tulips, hyacinths, lillies, &c., have died down in August, and these, with iris, should be reset immediately, if a new bed is wanted. Set out evergreens, if a ball can be removed with them.

The Rocky Mountain Douglas fir is a native evergreen found in the Trans-Pecos area of West Texas; it is used primarily for timber. Native East Texas conifers include Eastern red-cedar and Bald cypress. Eastern red-cedar is used for fence posts and cedar chests, as its oil acts as a natural insect repellant. Bald cypress occurs in rivers and swamps; it is best known for its knobby "knees," which act as additional support for the tree in its watery environment.

1

Pine needle bundles,
native East Texas conifers   2

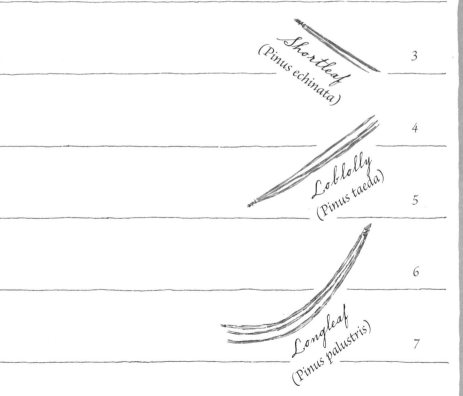

Shortleaf
(Pinus echinata)   3

Loblolly
(Pinus taeda)   4

5

Longleaf
(Pinus palustris)   6

7

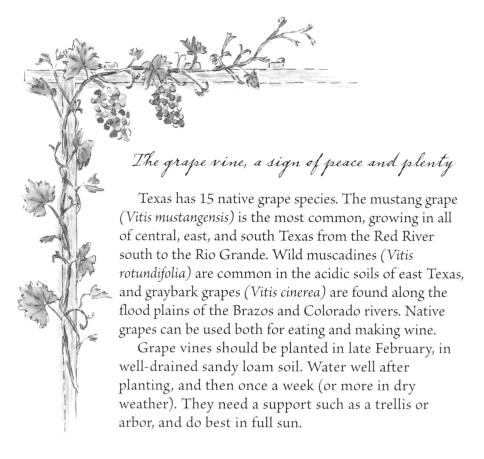

The grape vine, a sign of peace and plenty

Texas has 15 native grape species. The mustang grape (*Vitis mustangensis*) is the most common, growing in all of central, east, and south Texas from the Red River south to the Rio Grande. Wild muscadines (*Vitis rotundifolia*) are common in the acidic soils of east Texas, and graybark grapes (*Vitis cinerea*) are found along the flood plains of the Brazos and Colorado rivers. Native grapes can be used both for eating and making wine.

Grape vines should be planted in late February, in well-drained sandy loam soil. Water well after planting, and then once a week (or more in dry weather). They need a support such as a trellis or arbor, and do best in full sun.

*Many of the early settlers went in
the fall to gather wild grapes and
plums, which made delicious jellies,
conserves, and deep-dish cobblers.*
—Mrs. C.G. Landis,
A Legacy of Words,
Texas Women's Stories 1850–1920

8

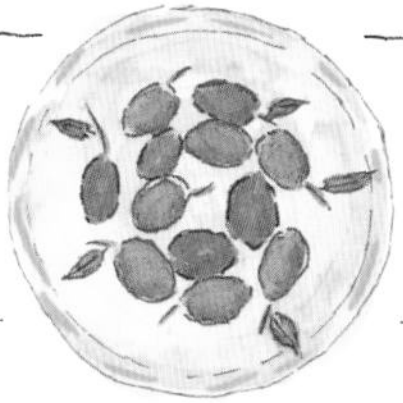

9

10

11

12

*In our family, having a glass of wine
was always for 'medicinal reasons.'*

13

14

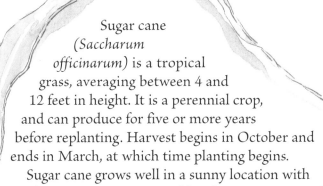

Sugar cane
(*Saccharum
officinarum*) is a tropical
grass, averaging between 4 and
12 feet in height. It is a perennial crop,
and can produce for five or more years
before replanting. Harvest begins in October and
ends in March, at which time planting begins.
Sugar cane grows well in a sunny location with
ample water. It is propagated by planting sections of the
stem, making sure that each
section contains at least
one node or joint.
These sections are
laid horizontally

in furrows. Sprouts will
appear at the nodes within
several weeks. After 7 to 8
months of growth, the canes are
ready to be harvested.
In the 19th century, sugar cane was grown
along the Gulf Coast and in East Texas; it is now grown
primarily in the Lower Rio Grande Valley.

15

*For a sweet treat, remove
the outer leaves, and chew.*

16

17

18

19

20

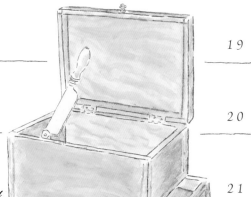

21

*Sugar box, c. 1900, for cutting
a sugar loaf into cubes*

Ruby-throated Hummingbird
(Archilochus colubris)

Millions of hummingbirds migrate through Texas during the summer and early fall, on their way to winter homes in Mexico and Central America. East Texas, the eastern Hill Country, and the Edwards Plateau are favorite stopovers for the Ruby-throated Hummingbird, and Austin or San Antonio and points west for Black-chinned Hummingbirds (A. alexandri). Broad-tailed (Selasphorus platycercus), Rufous (S. rufus), and Calliope (Stellula calliope) hummingbirds prefer the "sky islands," tall mountains surrounded by the Chihuahuan Desert, that are located west of the Pecos River.

The hummingbird's name comes from the sound made by the beating of its wings, an impressive 40 to 80 beats/second. These tiny acrobats can hover, fly forward, backward, sideways, and even upside down.

Their average weight is 3 grams (0.1 ounces), and it will double before they continue on their migratory flight. Some, though few, choose a sea route, flying 600 miles over the Gulf of Mexico. Most opt for a longer land route, following the Gulf Coast south into Mexico and beyond. Cruising speed is 30 mph, with bursts up to 60 mph when heading toward a meal of nectar or insects. A hummingbird laps up nectar with a tongue that extends beyond the tip of the beak.

A cup-shaped nest is made from a spider web and camouflaged with bits of lichen. It can expand to accomodate nestlings' growth spurts.

22

Autumnal, or fall equinox: September 22
or 23, depending on the year.
        —The Old Farmer's 2007 Almanac

23

24

25

26

27

28

Most hummingbirds lay two white eggs, each about the size of a pea.

In 19th century Texas, the principal staple crops were corn and cotton. Cotton was the cash crop, and corn was used mostly for consumption by the family and their animals. With relatively little cultivation, corn grew well in the rich soil stretching from the Gulf of Mexico to the Red River.

Corn on the cob, cornbread, tortillas, spoon bread, hush puppies; in one form or another, corn was, and is, a basic item of Texans' diet.

Corn and pumpkins are harvested last.

About two years after we moved to Floydada, my
husband brought a grist mill into the town, and people for
miles around would come in to have their milo, maize, corn
and other grains ground into meal. The grist mill was run
with the wind, and we did business when the wind blew.
—Mrs. Arthur B. Duncan,
A Legacy of Words, Texas Women's Stories 1850–1920

SEPTEMBER

*The metate (grinding slab) and mano (grinding stone)
were used for grinding corn, nuts, and berries.*

GARDEN CALENDAR

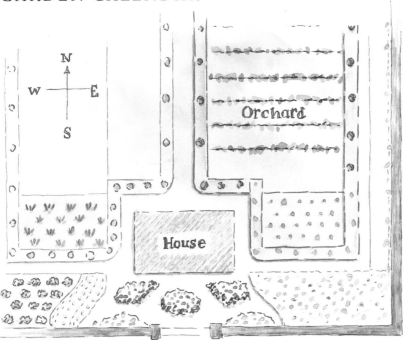

Lay off young orchard grounds now, and break up the same without delay. Dig holes for shade trees, and let them remain open until the soil pulverizes. Make boxwood borders. Sage, thyme, rosemary, &c., may be reset.

We may have light frosts about the 20th, but little ice before November or December. Tomato vines can be gathered and stored away for two weeks, and the fruit then gathered and house-ripened like apples.

Boxwood
(Buxus microphylla)

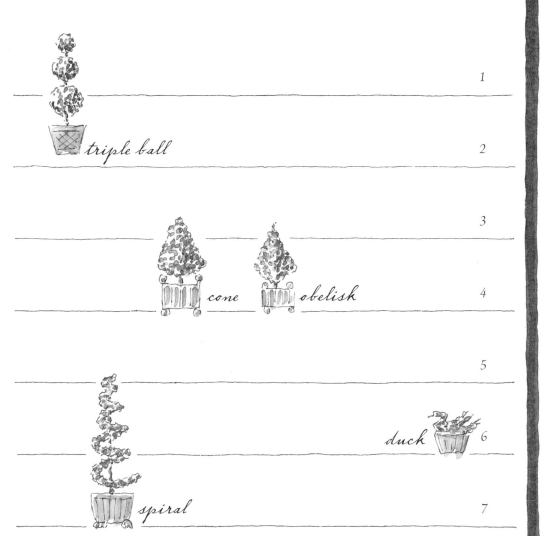

triple ball

cone *obelisk*

duck

spiral

1

2

3

4

5

6

7

The row of Victorian buildings on Main Street, downtown Houston, was built around 1880 in Italianate style.

With the arrival of the railroad in 1853, Houston's role as a business and commercial center increased. Cotton was its main source of income in those early days, followed by sugar, and early vegetables for Northern markets. Further expansion came with the construction of the ship channel in the 1870s, and its role then changed from river town to inland seaport.

8

9

10

11

12

*The names of the proprietors often appeared
in the upper portion of the façade.*

13

14

A BRIEF HISTORY OF GINGERBREAD

Porch brackets, Piney Point (Houston), c. 1848

Gingerbread was a product of the Industrial Revolution, which allowed elaborate ornamentation to be turned or cut by a lathe or jigsaw. It was used primarily in the Victorian style, to ornament columns, banisters, galleries, and the roof soffit, or undersurface, below the gables. It was also added as an embellishment to existing structures. Fishscale shingles, often used in the gable end, were another form of decoration used during the Victorian era.

15

16

17

18

19

Porch brackets, Westmoreland   20
(Houston), date unknown

21

2 2

2 3

2 4

2 5

2 6

2 7

2 8

Fretwork spandrels, Georgetown, c. 1895

29

30

*Fretwork spandrels, Marlin,
date unknown*

31

Gable brackets, Marlin, date unknown

GARDEN CALENDAR

This is the best season to set out fruit trees, grape vines, small fruits, roses, flowering shrubs, &c. Before the leaves open in spring, young roots will have been formed from one to three inches long. Set out strawberries—but the dewberry is more reliable and profitable. These and blackberries bear the first year; grapes the next, and then come peaches, pears and apples. For strawberries, prepare the land well by deep plowing, and lay the rows off three feet wide. Cut off all runners, mulch well with straw or hay just before the berries set, and you will not fail.

Brazos Blackberry

Plant strawberries with roots spread out in a fan shape. Barely cover the crown.

dewberry

strawberry

raspberry

1

2

3

4

5

6

7

Pecan trees (*Carya illinoensis*) are native to creek and river bottoms, and appreciate full sun and soil that is deep, fertile, and well-drained. They have a substantial root system, and do best when planted at least 35 feet apart. A minimum of five years is required before a tree begins to bear nuts; it can then produce for several hundred years.

There are currently more than 1,000 varieties of pecan trees; some are better suited for landscaping, and others as a source of nuts.

"Paccan" was used by the Algonquin Indians to designate a nut that must be cracked with a stone. The pecan became the state tree in 1919.

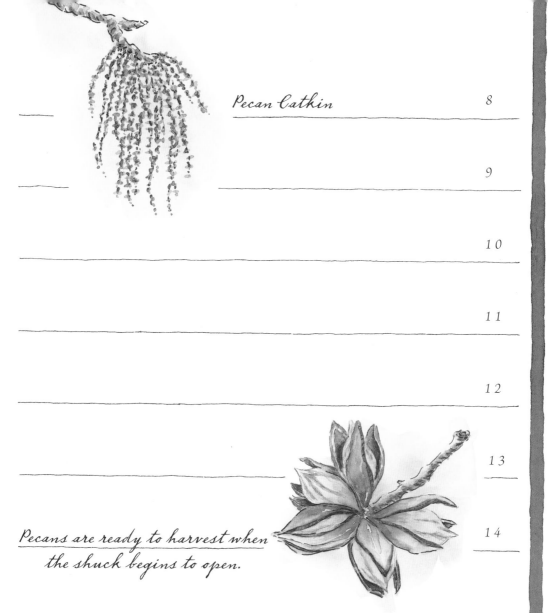

Pecan Catkin

8

9

10

11

12

13

14

Pecans are ready to harvest when
the shuck begins to open.

SAM H. RAHL & CO.
WOOL & MOHAIR

WOOL WAREHOUSE

For business, travel, or pleasure,

McANELLY'S DRY GOODS

HOUSTON 93 MILES — MAGNOLIA — FORT WORTH 205 MILES

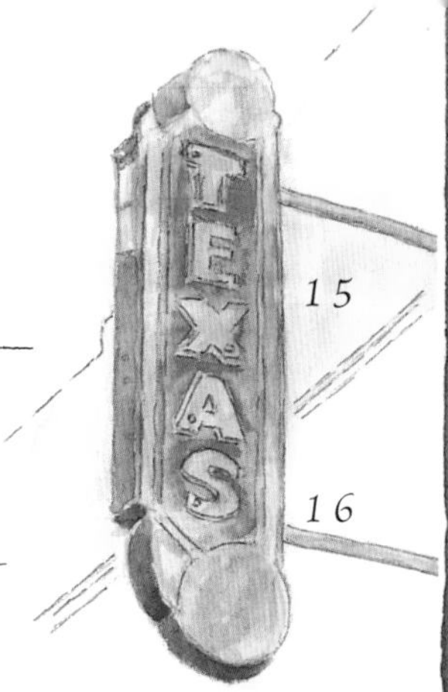
TEXAS

15

16

signs were everywhere.

17

18

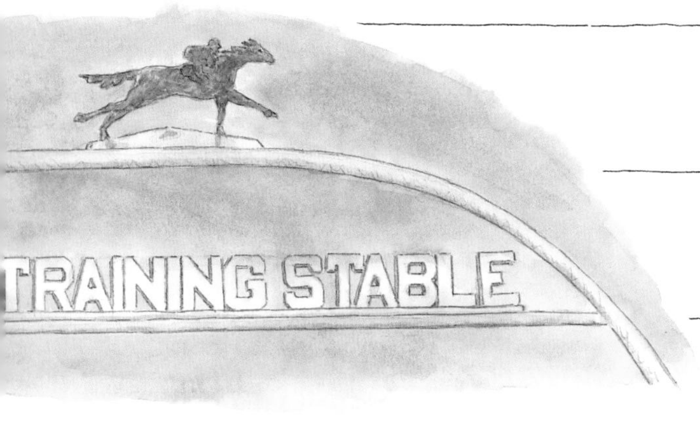
TRAINING STABLE

19

20

21

NOVEMBER

Storekeepers were considered to be the mainstay of early communities. Most stores quickly became general mercantile establishments, [and] to step inside [one] was a world within itself. First came a feeling of dimness and gloom due to no lighting and the heavily-laden shelves and tables with narrow aisles between. There was the smell of plug tobacco, just cut; coffee, just ground; onions hanging in bags along the wall; the unforgettable aroma of new leather just made into saddles, boots, and belts; the musty-tang of bolt after bolt of dress materials; and the sweet appetizing delight of peppermint candy sticks. Arranged at different places over the store were kegs and barrels of all sizes. They were brimming with sugar, flour, vinegar, pickles, salt, molasses, nails, and bolts. Toward the back was the hardware department and all the wares the early-day housewife could ask for.

At about the center of the store was the most important place of all, for there stood the pot-bellied stove. It was around this stove that people of the community were inevitably drawn to visit. The storekeeper became the civic leader, barterer, confidant, and public creditor. When times were hard and no rains came, the storekeeper became the one person in the community people turned to for credit and help. He listened to every farmer's woes—every person's illnesses, political views, and arguments.

Some stayed for a short time, while others spent a great part of their lives 'keeping the store.'
—Hartal Blackwell, *Mills County—the Way It Was*

22

23

24

25

26

27

There was usually a bench or a few chairs close to the front door where the ladies sat together and chatted about the ills of their children, how their gardens grew, and perhaps complimented each other on a new calico dress or a ruffled bonnet.
—Hartal Blackwell,
Mills County—the Way It Was

28

NO IDLE HANDS

Young girls began to learn needlework at an early age. Dutifully and laboriously, they practiced an assortment of stitches and recorded them on samplers. These samplers had cross-stitched alphabets and pious verses such as "Here the needle plies its busy task." They were often dated and signed by the artist. One young lady added her own message: "Patty Polk did this and she hated every stitch she did in it. She loves to read much more."

While their mother was sewing, a button box kept little ones occupied finding matching pairs, sorting by colors, and learning to count. A game of "Hide the thimble" was another pastime. An older sibling or available aunt would hide the thimble, then give "hot" and "cold" clues when they were near or far away.

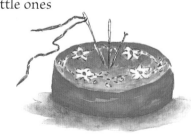

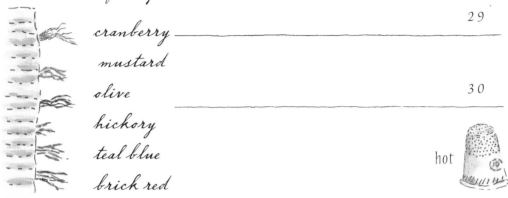

A selection of sampler colors:

cranberry _____ 29

mustard

olive _____ 30

hickory

teal blue

brick red

hot

is just

why that baby

cute as a button

cold

GARDEN CALENDAR

About the 25th we may expect steady cold weather. The winter garden is already planted, and the great work of this month is to prepare for the spring crop, and to protect half-hardy vegetables and young tender roses, verbenas, carnations, &c. Nothing is better than a light covering of oak leaves. It is only our sleeting northers that we need dread.

Continue to plant fruit trees, but do not expose the roots to winds or frosts. Make cuttings of grapes, quinces, roses, honeysuckles, altheas, &c., &c. Remove old wood from blackberries, raspberries, roses, &c.

In cold frames, continue to sow beets, lettuce, celery, onions, cabbage, cauliflower, borecole, and hardy flowery seeds, for transplanting in spring.

Peach seeds kept in moist soil can be planted now.

1

_____

Year of snow
Fruit will grow
—Eats, a Folk History
of Texas Foods

2

_____

3

_____

4

_____

5

_____

6

_____

7

_____

DECEMBER

WEATHER EVENTS

Tornado

Storm Surge

Sleet

Downpour

Hurricane

Norther

Diversity of weather in Texas results from its location between the warm waters of the Gulf of Mexico and the high plateaus and mountains in the north and west. Temperatures have dipped as low as -23 in both Tulia (1899) and Seminole (1933), and climbed to 120 in Seymour (1936). The year with the most amount of rainfall for the state was in 1900 (42 inches), and the least in 1917 (14 inches).* Cold snaps, downpours, blizzards, and tornadoes, one only has to wait a bit for a new weather event to come along.

*Dates quoted are from 1820 to 1950.

They [northers] most frequently occur after a few days of damp dull weather, and generally about once a fortnight. Their approach is known by a dark bank rising on the horizon, and gradually overspreading the heavens. The storm bursts forth with wonderful suddenness and tremendous violence, and generally lasts forty-eight hours; the wind after that period veers round to the east and southward, and the storm gradually abates. During the continuance of a norther, the cold is intense, and the wind so penetrating, it is almost impossible to keep oneself warm.

—Matilda Charlotte Houstoun, *Texas and the Gulf of Mexico; or, Yachting in the New World,* 1845

8

9

1 0

1 1

1 2

1 3

1 4

CHRISTMAS PREPARATIONS

Ladies of the home, from old to young, had been busy with their needles and thread stringing garlands of pop-corn for draping the tree. Strings of knitting yarn were sometimes wound together to make a colorful decoration.

Pop-corn balls were made several days in advance, creating an effective decoration hanging against the deep green of the tree, and were delicious for eating afterwards.

There was always plenty of sousemeat, spare-ribs, tenderloin, hams and sausage as hogs were killed before Christmas if the weather cooperated.

Pies, cakes, and candies were cooked several days in advance, and young appetites grew keen with anticipation as the aroma of mincemeat and syrup pies, chocolate cake and gingerbread drifted through the house.

—Hartal Blackwell, *Mills County—the Way It Was*

15

16

Cooking of the taffy began right away, and there was much laughter and fun as the pulling and breaking of the candy took place.
—Hartal Blackwell, *Mills County—the Way It Was*

17

18

19

20

Winter solstice: December 21 or 22, depending on the year.
—*The Old Farmer's 2007 Almanac*

21

HERE AT LAST

The most exciting event was the hanging of the Christmas stockings which covered the fireplace mantle, as most families were large. If there was no fireplace in the house, the stockings were hung on the foot of the bed. They were black ribbed cotton stockings for boys and girls, and Santa seemed to like them fine, for he filled them with sugar candy sticks, fruits, dolls for the girls, and tops and marbles for the boys.

Relatives gathered at one home for the Christmas dinner, and it wasn't unusual for thirty or thirty-five people to be there. All tables in the house were set, and children ate in the kitchen. If grandparents were present, they were seated at the head of the table, being honored guests, and a grandfather always said the Christmas blessing.

In later years, fireworks were added to the Christmas stockings, and were enjoyed by every child. Sparklers were delightful. Everyone waited until dark, then went into the cold Christmas night to shoot fire-crackers and Roman candles. Most will never forget the first Roman candle as it soared into the air and burst into beautiful colors against the darkened sky.

Toys in the early days were usually wind-up animals or clowns, small banks, celluloid and bisque dolls, tops and marbles.

—Hartal Blackwell, *Mills County—the Way It Was*

22

*An orange or an apple was
given to every child, and for some,
this was to be the last fresh fruit
they would see until summer.*
            —Hartal Blackwell,
Mills County—the Way It Was

23

24

25

26

The company makes the feast.
—The Old Farmer's 2007 Almanac

27

28

In our family, my father would invite friends, neighbors, and business associates over for a glass of eggnog on New Year's Eve. Mother brought out her punch bowl for the occasion, and was in charge of ladling the eggnog into the delicate, transparent cups.

—Kathryn Cavitt's journal

Eggnog

$^1/_3$ cup sugar
2 egg yolks
4 cups milk
2 egg whites
3 tablespoons sugar
1 teaspoon vanilla
Ground nutmeg
Rum

American Mistletoe (Phoradendron serotinum)

Beat $^1/_3$ cup sugar into egg yolks, stir in milk. Cook over medium heat, stirring constantly, until mixture coats a spoon. Add vanilla and chill 3 to 4 hours. Just before serving, beat egg whites until foamy. Gradually add 3 tablespoons of sugar, beating to soft peaks.

When serving, pour a bit of rum into a glass (for those so inclined), add the milk mixture, and top with a scoop of egg whites and a dash of nutmeg.

Serve black-eyed peas on New Year's Day
for good luck throughout the year.

Hopping John

6 slices of bacon, chopped
1 onion, chopped fine
1 cup black-eyed peas
4 tomatoes, diced

1 green pepper, chopped
2 cloves garlic, halved
1 bay leaf
2 ribs celery, chopped
4 sprigs of fresh thyme
Cayenne pepper

Cook bacon in a Dutch oven over medium heat until crisp. Add onion and sauté until translucent. Wash peas, and add to bacon-onion mixture, along with 3–4 cups of water. Add remaining ingredients except the cayenne pepper, and simmer until tender, adding water if necessary. Season to taste with cayenne, and serve over rice, with cornbread on the side.

When shelling black-eyed peas,
nine peas in a pod
bring good luck.

DECEMBER

Paramount Star

Spinning Stars

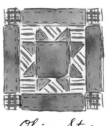

Ohio Star

NOTES

Cross-stitch motifs from a
sampler completed in West
Texas in the 1880s.

Variable
Star

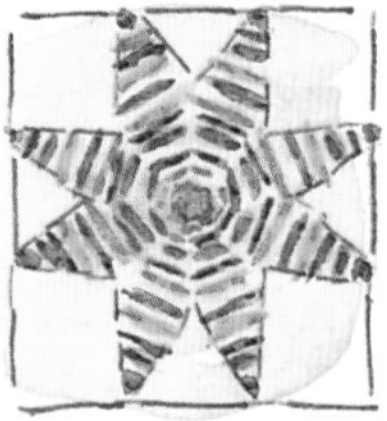

String-
pieced Star

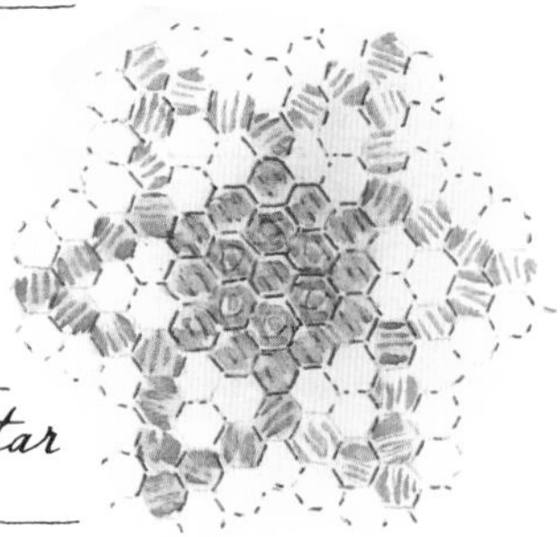

Mosaic Star

Star
of the East

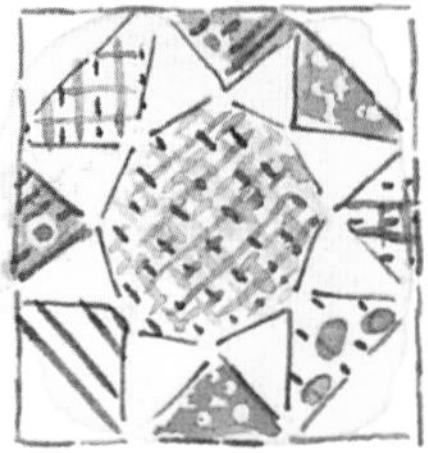

Evening Star

BIBLIOGRAPHY

prickly

Banks, McMillan. *The New Texas Reader.* San Antonio, Texas: Naylor Company, 1960.

Blackwell, Hartal Langford. *Mills County—the Way It Was.* Goldthwaite, Texas: The Eagle Press, 1976.

Boland, Maureen and Bridget. *Old Wives' Lore for Gardeners.* New York: Farrar, Straus and Giroux, 1976.

Bolton, Ethel Stanwood and Coe, Eva Johnston. *American Samplers.* Boston: Thomas Todd Company, 1921.

A Book of Tested Recipes Arranged by the Woman's Missionary Society of the Methodist Church, McGregor, Texas, 1920.

Bowditch, Nathaniel. *American Practical Navigator.* Washington, D.C.: Government Printing Office, 1926.

Bresenhan, Karoline. *Lone Stars, a Legacy of Texas Quilts, 1836–1936.* Austin, Texas: University of Texas Press, 1986.

Bresenhan, Karoline. *Lone Stars, a Legacy of Texas Quilts, 1936–1986.* Austin, Texas: University of Texas Press, 1990.

Burke, James. *Burke's Texas Almanac and Immigrant's Handbook for 1879* (a facsimile reproduction of the 1879 edition). Austin, Texas: Steck-Warlick Company, 1969.

Carter, Kathryn Turner. *Stagecoach Inns of Texas.* Waco, Texas: Texian Press, 1972.

Chambers, Robert. *Chambers's Book of Days; a miscellany of popular antiquities in connection with the calendar, including anecdote, biography, & history, curiosities of literature and oddities of human life and character.* London: W. & R. Chambers, 1879.

Cowper, William. *The Task.* London: Printed for J. Johnson, 1785.

Dresel, Gustav. *Gustav Dresel's Houston Journal: Adventures in North America and Texas, 1837–1841.* Translated by Max Freund. Austin, Texas: University of Texas Press, 1954.

Echols, Gordon. *Early Texas Architecture.* Fort Worth, Texas: Texas Christian University Press, 2000.

Garrett, J. Howard. *Texas Organic Vegetable Gardening.* Houston, Texas: Gulf Publishing Company, 1999.

Gray, Asa M.D. *How Plants Grow, a Simple Introduction to Structural Botany with a Popular Flora, or an Arrangement and Description of Common Plants both Wild and Cultivated.* New York: American Book Company, 1858.

Hafertepe, Kenneth. *Abner Cook, Master Builder on the Texas Frontier.* Austin, Texas: Texas State Historical Association, 1991.

Haley, James L. *Texas, an Album of History.* New York, Doubleday & Company, 1985.

Haslam, Gillian. *A Herbal Book of Days.* New York: Quadrillion Publishing Inc., 1993.

Harris, Coy F. ed. *Windmill Tales*. Lubbock, Texas: Texas Tech University Press, 2004.

Houghton, Dorothy Knox Howe et al. *Houston's Forgotten Heritage*. College Station, Texas: Texas A & M University Press, 1998.

Houstoun, Matilda Charlotte, *Texas and the Gulf of Mexico; or Yachting in the New World* (a facsimile reproduction of the 1845 edition). Austin, Texas: Steck-Warlick Company, 1969.

Kowert, Elise. *Old Homes and Buildings of Fredericksburg*. Fredericksburg, Texas: Fredericksburg Publishing Company, 1977.

Linck, Ernestine Sewell. *Eats, a Folk History of Texas Foods*. Fort Worth, Texas: Texas Christian University Press, 1989.

Mills, Ava E. ed. *A Legacy of Words, Texas Women's Stories, 1850–1920*. San Angelo, Texas: Doss Books, 1999.

Mills, Betty J. *Calico Chronicle, Texas Women and their Fashions, 1830–1910*. Lubbock, Texas: Texas Tech University Press, 1985.

Old Farmer's 2007 Almanac, The. Dublin, NH: Yankee Publishing Incorporated, 2006.

Ramsey, Bets. *Southern Quilts: Surviving Relics of the Civil War*. Nashville, Tennessee: Rutledge Hill Press, 1998.

Richardson, Rupert N. *Texas, the Lone Star State*. Englewood Cliffs, New Jersey: Prentice Hall Inc., 1958.

Ring, Betty. *Needlework, an Historical Survey*. New York: Main Street/Universe Books, 1975.

Rogers, Lisa Waller. *A Texas Sampler.* Lubbock, Texas: Texas Tech University Press, 1998.

Slatta, , Richard W. *The Cowboy Encyclopedia*. New York and London: W. W. Norton & Company, 1994.

Stevens, Frances. *The Usages of the Best Society*. New York: A.L. Burt, 1884.

Texas Almanac. Dallas, Texas: Dallas Morning News, 1964.

Yabsley, Suzanne. *Texas Quilts, Texas Women*. College Station, Texas: Texas A & M University Press, 1984.

Handbook of Texas Online,
    s.v. "CATTLE TRAILING"
    http://www.tsha.utexas.edu/handbook/online/articles/CC/avc1.html
    (accessed August 26, 2006)
    s.v. "FREDERICKSBURG, TX"
    http://www.tsha.utexas.edu/handbook/online/articles/FF/hff3.html
    (accessed January 16, 2006)

bayou

moss

spanish

alligator

s.v. "GOODNIGHT, CHARLES"
http://www.tsha.utexas.edu/handbook/online/articles/GG/fgo11.html
(accessed August 25, 2006)
s.v. "GULF OF MEXICO"
http://www.tsha.utexas.edu/handbook/online/articles/GG/rrg7.html
(accessed April 4, 2007)
s.v. "WINDMILLS"
http://www.tsha.utexas.edu/handbook/online/articles/WW/aow1.html
(accessed January 17, 2007)
s.v. "URBANIZATION"
http://www.tsha.utexas.edu/handbook/online/articles/UU/hyunw.html
(accessed June 21, 2007)

Lipe, John A., Larry Stein, George Ray McEachern, John Begnaud, and Sammy Helmers. "Home Fruit Production—Pecans." Texas Cooperative Extension, Texas A&M University, http://aggie-horticulture.tamu.edu/extension/homefruit/pecan/pecan.html

McEachern, George Ray, Larry Stein, and Jim Kamas. "Growing Pierces's Disease Resistant Grapes in Central, South and East Texas." Texas Cooperative Extension, Texas A&M University (March 6, 1997), http://aggie-horticulture.tamu.edu/extension/fruit/piercegrapes/pdr.html

Welch, William C. "Southern Magnolia (Magnolia grandiflora)." Texas Cooperative Extension, Texas A&M University (July–August 2005),
http://aggiehorticulture.tamu.edu/extension/newsletters/hortupdate/julaug,5/Magnolia.html

Grapes
http://aggie-horticulture.tamu.edu/southerngarden/Texaswine.html
http://aggie-horticulture.tamu.edu/extension/fruit/piercegrapes/pdr.html

Pecans
http://aggie-horticulture.tamu.edu/extension/homefruit/pecan/pecan.html

winter

sky

and

fields

ACKNOWLEDGMENTS

First and foremost, our heartfelt appreciation to Rue Judd and the staff at Bright Sky Press for their vision, enthusiasm, insight, and encouragement.

oleander

sea

sand dollar

Sincere thanks to the following individuals and museums for their contributions to the art and architecture portions of the book: Susan Judd Brown, George Anne Cormier (Calhoun County Museum), Mary Frances Couper, Tanya L. Meadows (American Wind Power Center), Mills County Historical Museum, Texas General Land Office.

A debt of gratitude to the following individuals and institutions for their patience and expertise in matters relating to flora and fauna: Burton Cotton Gin and Museum; Paul Hammerschmidt, Bob Murphy (Texas Parks and Wildlife Department, Coastal Fisheries Division); Dwight Harkey (Texas A&M Agricultural Service); Mark Klym, Cliff Shackelford (Texas Parks and Wildlife Department, Wildlife Division); Tamilee Nennich (Texas A&M University); Anita Tiller (Mercer Arboretum and Botanic Gardens); Damon E. Waitt (Lady Bird Johnson Wildflower Center).

distant

hills

limestone

mesquite

Material for cuisine (both the kitchen itself, as well as style of cooking), resultant recipes, and traditions large and small have come to us from previous generations of Andersons and Bruces, in particular Ione Clark Anderson and Fannie Beeson Bruce. We are also grateful to both families for letters saved, journals written, scrapbooks composed, stories told, and babies patted … a glimpse of who we are, and whence we've come.

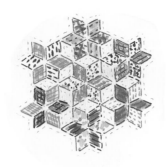

With the Seven Sisters,
we take our leave.